IN THE CHALK CIRCLE

• CIVILISED BOOKS •
GREENWICH VILLAGE, NY

IN THE
CHALK CIRCLE

Poems from Washington Square

B.F. SPÄTH

• CIVILISED BOOKS •

GREENWICH VILLAGE, NY

I am a rational man. A down-to-earth man, with a firm grasp on things. Is this true? No, it isn't—these are merely words that lay flat on the page. They sit there, obtuse, obedient, and matter-of-fact ...

THE GOLDEN AGE OF THE CITY

In those days, every step, every gesture, every event, no matter how minor, was fraught with meaning, magic, and possessed of a monumental grandeur. Ah! How far we have fallen from those days ...

HOLLOW MORNING

My friends had fallen away—one-by-one—and on a hollow morning in early summer, I found myself alone in the dark confines of my tenement apartment. A morbid fear crept over me, accompanied by the conviction that life was occurring elsewhere. Unease drove me out into the sunlight, where I stood, transfixed. Fearful of attracting attention, I wandered away, with no destination in mind, but there soon came over me a gathering awareness of Washington Square...

HIGH SUMMER

Obscured by ancient trees and foliage, it is not until one reaches the statue of Garibaldi, that the spectacle of the fountain erupts: by turns ecstatic, sombrous, and sublime, as it spouts into the heavy air of a High Summer afternoon in Washington Square Park.

THE SUNKEN PLAZA

Under the sway of a divine plant, I descended the three concrete steps into the Old Sunken Plaza of Washington Square, where, among the initiates, felt myself to be in *The Neighborhood of the Gods*.

HISTORIC SECTION

In a historic section of Washington Square Park, I listened politely, as a man grabbed me by the collar, and in a single breath, recounted the entire *History of Persia!*

LOST FOUNTAIN OBSERVANCES

When the fountain's turned off at day's end, such a solemn note is struck, that a tremor often passes through me, and through a silent, trembling park.

INSUBSTANTIAL SUBURB

On a numberless day, in an insubstantial suburb of Washington Square, I lingered on a phantom bench with not quite enough empirical evidence to support belief in my own existence.

AVENUE OF THE KINGS

But by night, by God! Washed by Jupiter and anointed by the Sun, I strode along the *Avenue of the Kings*, impervious to insult and innuendo, and intent on grabbing a portion of what is mine!

THE HOURS

Over the course of a ten months-long lull in my employment, grappling with an innate intransigence, I languished in a temporary office in an out-of-the-way warren in Washington Square Park, where I sat confounded, counting out *The Hours.*

EVERY THIRD DAY

Weakened by a mild form of malaria that breaks out in the bars and restaurants every third day, and under the patronage of a deity which we cannot at this time identify, I lay flat upon a scabrous bench in Washington Square Park, in the shade, where I practiced *The Abracadabra of Everyday Life*.

ALL THE COLORS

As the sun went down one more time, it pulled all the discarded scraps of conversation with it, all the *Insults, Threats, and Boasts* that hung in the air, all the burdens, jokes, and joys, and all the colors—until there was nothing left: Who has ever seen such a misfortune?

OCCULT NOTEBOOK

I kept returning to Washington Square—day after day—as if I were an archeologist, hoping to excavate the secrets buried beneath the surface—as if the *Everyday Reality* of the park was not good enough!

INTERIOR

Yesterday I was exploring the murky interior of *Journal No. 31,* hoping to locate some useful information about myself, some hint as to how I might proceed—but all I found were wheedling complaints, intolerance of my fellow man, and a preternatural obsession with the minutest changes in the weather!

AMORPHOUS AFTERNOON

In the fading light of a late-afternoon, in the Autumn of the year, I found myself upon a bench in a neglected suburb of Washington Square, and as the shadow of evening covered the park, I compiled an inventory of my *Spiritual Strengths and Weaknesses*.

ALONE, BY NIGHT

With continuous and gloomy introspection, across the deserted pages of certain solemn books, alone, by night, I pondered the chronicles of a park, the soil of which is no longer available for examination ...

PROTO-RELIGION

As I sat in the Chess Circle, amid rhythmic chants and rank suffumigations, I was reminded that spiritual practice, sorcery, and medicine are often closely intertwined.

UNDER SODIUM

Under the callous light of a sodium lamp in Washington Square, I put my thoughts upon a page: What is, what was, and what should have been!

EVERY WICKED CORNER

Blown to bits by an ordinary conversation, I fled at once to every wicked corner of the park, where I sat in sorrow, and tried to reconstruct myself from scratch.

OVER THE PARK

As the shadow of evening passed over the park, the fountain spray collapsed, and though a wondrous mystic mood prevailed, the crowd seemed unaware.

FUNERAL TRAIN

As I counted out the minutes of a mournful sleepless night, my past ran by before me like some endless funeral train ...

DEMONICAL DREAM

On an evening of unusual magnetic activity, mazed and muttering obscenities half-aloud, I saw myself descending Washington Square West, pursued by a certain demonical dream suffered two nights previous.

RIGHT THE HELL

A stiff head-wind of misfortune blew me right the hell into Washington Square, where I walked among the people, and took the minutes of the park.

ANTAGONISTIC PLANET

Under strange goings on in the heavens, amid intimations of magnetic disturbance, and caught by the pull of an antagonistic planet, I walked as if in a dream into the Chess Circle, where I was welcomed as a dear friend, and ushered onto a waiting bench.

MIDNIGHT STATION

In a midnight station, trapped below the streets, through grinding gears, and metal bars, I struggled to escape the dreadful scaffolds of the self.

THE NOCTURNAL DOORSTEP

I am challenged by fragments of myself—they often come to me on *The Nocturnal Doorstep*—they're here to accuse and harass me, of course, but also to fight for their lives!

SACRAMENT

In a heretical section of Washington Square Park, as I made communion with a magical plant, I recalled that it was from such inauspicious beginnings that most of *The World's Great Religions* were born.

THE REMAINDER OF THE DAY

It is worth noting that Washington Square is fickle: even though the park is un-gated, I am often denied entrance, and will spend *The Remainder of the Day* and evening wandering the periphery, gazing sadly at the festivities within.

ANNOTATED AFTERNOON

2:09 p.m.—Washington Square Park
Beautiful afternoon in a dream—soon to be nothing but
A Lost Page in a barbaric book: Days squandered and turned
to paper…

AGITATED CALENDAR

On an isolated evening, in an area of Washington Square that had fallen into disuse, and no longer appeared on any map, I found myself consulting an agitated calendar, where all the lucky and unlucky days had been stamped in red and blue!

THE RUINS OF CIRCINIUM

As I wandered through the *Ruins of Circinium*, past a pantheon of deities that embodied torpor, delirium, and decline, I caught the whiff of a magical plant, whose aroma is pleasing to the Gods...

APARTMENT NUMBER ONE

Cumbered by misfortune, and hounded by *Oracles & Omens*, I called upon an inner strength, and thus fortified, continued to pay rent on the atmospheric sarcophagus of *Apartment No.1*.

THE SPÄTH COAT OF ARMS

In order to level the playing field, and gain parity with my foes, I hereby announce that any future correspondence from me shall bear the stamp of the official *Späth Coat of Arms*. So be it!

TOWNSHIPS OF MAGNESIA

And though by night I roamed the fabled townships of Magnesia: Glaphyrae, Borshyria, Olizon, and Boebe, by day—Alas!—I trod the same surface as the tourists, and breathed the selfsame airs.

CONTEMPLATION

On an afternoon of no consequence, in the waning days of August, I found myself upon a paralytic bench in the north east quadrant of Washington Square, engulfed in the rank miasma of the adjacent Dog Run, where I contemplated a move to a different bench ... perhaps somewhere in the southwest section of the park ...

MAPS OF THE PERIOD

On the sunken Isle of Manhattan, in an area known as Greenwich Village, there once existed—if maps of the period are to be taken seriously—the extraordinary conjunction of West 4th and West 10th streets!

QUESTIONABLE CALENDAR

During the milky ascent of a swollen Summer Moon intent on mischief, on a questionable calendar, and with strange goings-on in the Financial District, I swayed precariously upon the rim of a water-filled ditch on a torn-up and desecrated Fulton Street.

SUBTERRANEAN FOUNTAIN

All about a Friday afternoon, in a park that had fallen off the map, I sat, crabbed and cantankerous, showering silent maledictions upon every passing tourist, tramp, and miscreant.

OFF-REGISTER RUMINATIONS

On an off-register afternoon, in the Autumn of the year, aggravated, and in the grip of a lingering malady, I found myself mired on a bench in an uncharted warren of Washington Square, where I turned the listless pages of *Notebook No. 35*, in search of a theory that would account for all human actions!

RE-APPEARING FACE

All around the city, in passing window panes, my face kept re-appearing, so I hurried on my way.

THE HOT SEASON

During the Hot Season, when the fevers run unchecked through Washington Square, when the chants of the Chess Circle take on a menacing malarial tone, when tempers burn and waters boil—this is when I find it high time to seek shelter under the shade of The Holy Bhang Leaf in the deepest interior of the park.

AS THE DAYS WORE DOWN

As the days wore down, and a strange *Barbaric Architecture* rose up around Washington Square, with muttered curses and complaints, I set out in search of a plant of both fibrous and intoxicating qualities.

IN A LAWLESS SUBURB

In a lawless suburb of Washington Square, under the very noses of the authorities, and at considerable risk to my person, I arranged a consultation with a magical plant of oracular properties, referred to in some districts as the Opener of Subterranean Fountains, and in others as the Brightener of the Royal Mind, and in still others as the Liberator of Sin: I refer, of course, to Cannabis Afghanica!

THE TISCH FOUNTAIN

Knowing that it is common sense to edge as close as one can to the main source of wealth and patronage, I clung to a parasitical bench near The Tisch Fountain in Washington Square Park.

UNNATURAL MONDAY

On an unnatural Monday in Washington Square, under the sway of a Cannabis/Morning Glory extract, my confidence swelled to an unnatural level, and prey to the megalomania that often overtakes *The Schizoid*, I ascended the steps of the Holley Monument, turned to the crowd, and delivered the following remarks:

> "Take heart, Gentlemen! The enemy has overplayed his hand, and a terrible justice will soon commence!"

ZODIACAL EVENING

On an evening of zodiacal significance, as a renegade moon rose over Washington Square, the remnants of the human race gathered under its skeletal rays. Seduced by this gloomy ceremonial, I partook of *The Most Holy Grass of the Arabs*, and with off-register ruminations, and incoherent prayer, once again plunged into the darkness of pseudo-mysticism.

BLASTED LANDSCAPE

As an evil and *Orpimental Evening* pressed down upon me, with no small vexation, I struggled to disentangle myself from the wreckage of Washington Square Park. But in the exposed trenches of that blasted landscape, I began to entertain the outlines of a fanatical hope: that one day an excavation might bring to the surface a great transcendent literature!

QUOTATIONS

As I bantered with a friendly crowd gathered around the fountain, at length they became aware that my speech was made up largely of quotations, and with shouts and mockery, soon drove me out of the park!

RECKLESS DREAM

Somewhere in the south of an ancient reckless dream, I broke the seal of *Notebook No. 7*, and brought a plague upon the park ...

AFFIRMATION

Over the span of many years, I learned to appreciate that each moment spent in Washington Square Park is unique, though of a certain stultifying sameness.

COMMERCE

When things are brought to a boil in the Chess Plaza, when strange and terrible chants erupt, when the hustlers pace like tigers, and blood seems sure to spill, this is when I console myself with the belief that the people of the Chess Plaza are more concerned with commerce than with making war!

NOT TOO BAD, REALLY

WEDNESDAY, JUNE 14
2:39 pm—Washington Square Park
Overcast, humid, but not too bad, really...

ACCRETION OF ERROR

As I walked out one afternoon, in pursuit of the
Indo-Aryan Soma, I was overtaken by an accretion of error,
and thrown off-course, blundered into a maudlin section of
Washington Square, where I sat, confounded amongst dogs,
children, and spinning acrobats!

A REAL PIECE OF JUNK

To a meeting of my peers, I dragged my *False Self System*, but it's a rickety-rackety mess: it doesn't work, it's moot, it's a real piece of junk!

EDGE OF THE FOUNTAIN

Through the surrounding streets, and into Washington Square, like an ominous and gathering cloud, my past pursued me, and at the *Edge of the Fountain*, grabbed me by the collar, and wrung out a confession!

THE SUNKEN AMPHITHEATER

At certain odd hours of the day and night, I find myself brooding upon the old Sunken Amphitheater in Washington Square, that destination that no longer exists. I saw mention of it in the despairing pages of *Journal No. 37*. The notebooks: the only things left!

NIGHT-WATCHMAN

In the wake of a three-month's long lull in my employment, in the waning days of December, I threw myself upon a pauper's bench in Washington Square, and resigned myself to penury. But a real man wouldn't trouble you with mewling complaints and niggling woes. A real man might simply seek employment as a messenger or night-watchman, pay his bills, and shut his trap! Aye! But if I were a real man, you would not now be turning the blighted pages of *The Chalk Circle!*

INTO THE STREETS

The rising and falling *Streets of Mesopotamia* had their origin in the citizen's habit of dumping their garbage out the windows and directly into the streets, where it was tamped down by a million footsteps, and baked under the merciless sun of Babylon, until it hardened into brick, and became a permanent fixture of the street grid.

UNKNOWN AFTERNOON

On an unknown afternoon, in the Old Parade Grounds of Washington Square, I found myself in a hypothetical state of mind, with no verbal equivalents, and though I marched shoulder-to-shoulder among the great swollen *Ranks of The Unemployed*, I nevertheless felt myself to be wholly alone.

60

PROCESSIONAL STREET

In those days, possessed of classical physique, and dark and gold-colored allure, I would daily parade along Processional Street, presenting so luminous and spectacular an arc, that I was oft-times mistaken for a comet!

THE FOUNTAIN

On a late-Summer afternoon of unusual luminescence, as *Dreams of Grandeur* settled upon Washington Square Park, having no pressing engagements or designs, I let go of myself, and surrendered to the ecstasies of the fountain.

SEISMIC REGION

During the whole of a fenced-off Friday, in a section of Washington Square marked for demolition, I sat marooned amid the rubble, riled, and well-stricken with spleen at finding myself in so feverishly seismic a region.

RAIN STREET

As I ran along Rain Street in a pelting Summer storm, my furtive, broken image watched me from the windows and the doors.

WHAT ABOUT A MAN?

What about a man who went outside without a self? Now that takes guts! Should he be lauded or condemned?

THE RUINS OF APHRODISIAS

Among the *Ruins of Aphrodisias*, I saw your shade upon
a spectral bench—Oh yes, I recall ... we sat there once,
together, in some shadowy insubstantial sphere.

ABOMINABLE REPUTATION

Another journal nears completion: a strange, murky, and savage record of *nothing!*—I'll soon throw it upon the stack. Ah! These modern books, how anemic they seem compared to the heroic *Books of Yesterday* ...

IN THE SEVENTH MONTH

In the seventh month of a seasonal lull in my employment, under the warm sun of Washington Square, I found myself upon a curious, hand-carved bench imported from Phoenicia, counting out the hours.

DISAGREEABLE BOOK

Sunlight burns across the pages of my journal: a certain *Notebook No. 37*, and that disagreeable book lies there upon my table, aflame...

MESSIANIC AFTERNOON

On an afternoon of messianic fervor, in a revolutionary frame of mind, I set out for Washington Square with the intention of breaching *The Great Wall* that separates each soul from another, but as I reached the rim of the fountain, a strange weakness of spirit crept upon me, and faltering, made the decision to abandon the entire project.

RUINS OF THE NIGHT

All along the length of my apartment, through the darkened closets of the night, like some abject, cringing hound, I crept, past forty statues of Nemesis, in as many *Sacred Shrines*.

ATLANTEAN DIARY

In the sunless aftermath of a Henbane mishap, as I felt my way through the darkness, my innermost secrets provided a strange form of illumination, allowing me to continue my study of *The Atlantean Hypothesis*.

CIRCUMNAVIGATION OF THE FOUNTAIN

In the twilight of a numberless day, as the apprehension of evening wore upon Washington Square Park, with ritual intent, I performed several circumnavigations of the fountain, and upon completion, was rewarded with the knowledge that man all too readily falls into *The Error of Vain Repetition*.

PAST THE FOUNTAIN

They're digging up Washington Square! All day and into a dreadful night, from one toxic bench to the next I fled. They pursued me past the fountain, and out the north-east gate—then through the twisting streets, and onto *The Nocturnal Doorstep*.

THE CLOCK RUNS DOWN

On a numberless day, not appearing on any calendar, bereft of *Aim and Ambition*, I languished upon a bench in a remote suburb of Washington Square, and in a snit, reviewed my options.

SULLIVAN AND THIRD

All around Washington Square, as I hurried through the ruined and rainy streets, only a step ahead of scandal and complaint, I was at last overtaken on the corner of Sullivan and Third, where a list of my indiscretions was thrust in my face!

WHAT ELSE?

Along the length of a single studied sentence, I addressed the questions of the self: Alright then—what else should I do?

A MAD CHRISTMAS

Two days before Christmas, as I wandered the deserted *Night Streets*, I came upon a homeless man of stern expression, seated like a king, high atop a throne of boxes, boards, and garbage bags, lit all around by blinking neon lights, the whole giving the impression of a great, glittering corruption.

ONEIRIC MERIDIAN

It was by way of one of the oneiric meridians that I was ushered into a spectral Washington Square Park, where I took notes on the many strange sights, and *Cyclopean Architecture*.

WASHINGTON SQUARE WEST

On an afternoon of the utmost malignancy, freshly mauled and mangled in the gears of an *Ordinary Conversation*, and persecuted by reality itself, I sought a measure of respite along that stinking stretch of pavement named Washington Square West, where I settled upon a decomposing bench, and resigned myself to whatever evils or apparitions might materialize in front of me.

INFERNAL INSTANT

My reflection and I saw each other at the same
infernal instant—we were both dismayed, and turned away:
I was the last person we wanted to see!

IN WASHINGTON SQUARE

Even here, in my natural habitat, I am a stranger, and what is worse, I have no understanding of the place—but on the other hand, I do have a role to play: as a disturber of *The Natural Order of Things!*

AUGUST SUN

In the Twelfth Month of a lull in my employment, as an August sun beat hard upon the park, a calculation proved beyond a doubt, that in two weeks time or less, my money would run out!

THEATRICAL MOON

In the thirteenth month of a lull in my employment, as I lay upon a bench, a bloated, mocking moon arose, and cursed me *While I Slept*.

ALL THROUGH WASHINGTON SQUARE

As a late-September evening crept upon the park, the fountain-spray collapsed, and a wondrous *Mystic Calm* prevailed, all through Washington Square.

ALL AT ONCE

All-at-once, I found myself on the corner of Mott & Mosco, in front of a Chinese apothecary: myriad roots, pills, powders, and potions sang out to me—I wanted to swallow them all—at once!

INTERSECTION

I find myself appearing spontaneously, perhaps on a street, or an intersection, briefly visible to the passersby, flickering uncertainly, clumsily, and then evaporating in a mist of *Guilt, Shame, and Confusion.*

ARTIFICIAL EVENING

Under painted constellations, in a gloomy circus tent, there hung a craven *Cardboard Moon* that watched me, and mocked my every step.

PERSONAL JOURNAL NO. I

In a competitive area of Washington Square, well aware that the real and the imaginary cannot co-exist, I retracted my lines of defense, and withdrew into a central citadel, where I recorded an entry in *Personal Journal No. 1*.

THE SARGASSO SEA

During the dog days in Washington Square, the Fountaineers often pump in waters from *The Sargasso Sea*, bringing with them the dreadful calm of that breezeless body of water.

CARELESS AFTERNOON

Under a thoughtless slap-dash sky, along a crudely-rendered street, I stopped to rest upon a cardboard bench, in a sketchy part of town.

AS FOR WASHINGTON SQUARE

As for Washington Square, I kept being called back—day after day—as if there were some mystery to be solved, some hidden truth that needed to be uncovered: The only mystery was why a man would delude himself into holding such beliefs!

CONVALESCENT PARK

During the whole of a pallid afternoon, in a convalescent section of Washington Square, I watched as tourists wandered about unconvincingly, like feeble articulations of myself, and in the process, sketched out the pale suggestion of an underworld.

STATIONARY BENCH

On a shapeless afternoon at the end of the calendar, I found myself upon a bench bolted into the asphalt of Washington Square, convinced that the whole machinery of living had come to a halt, and no amount of prayer or supplication could set it in motion once again.

WHAT ABOUT A MAN?

What about a man who turned his spleen upon himself, and ground himself to dust? What should we do about such a man?

DISCONCERTING LANDSCAPE

In a condemned section of the park, I sat and counted out the minutes—and indeed, it wasn't too long before the blow-torches hissed & sputtered, the jackhammers set up a terrible racket, and with the noise of twenty devils, a pavement cutter tore open the crust of Washington Square Park.

THE RUINS OF BORSHYRAE

Under a yoke of indifferent stars and hostile planets, beset by wild dogs and pigs, and holding in my hand the ground plan of a temple, I wandered, nightly, alone, through *The Ruins of Borshyrae.*

THE COLORATION OF BABYLON

In a parochial section of Washington Square, in the aftermath of a prolonged malady, by chance I came upon an exotic plant, and under its restorative powers, I grew young again, and my dreams took on *The Coloration of Babylon.*

SCATTERED PRAYERS

On a hi-jacked calendar, amidst scattered *Prayers and Lamentations*, the Old Park was finally smashed down into a ruin so complete that one can scarce believe it ever existed!

SOUTH OF THE FOUNTAIN

All along a rigamarole morning, in a sing-song section of Washington Square, I sat alone, by choice, because the company of even the most *Remarkable Men* soon becomes laborious.

MEGAPHONIC PARK

In a megaphonic section of Washington Square, mauled & mangled by the everyday activities of the park, I lay back on a blistered bench, and condemned *The Artificial Merriment of the Crowd.*

ACROSS WASHINGTON SQUARE

From across Washington Square, I heard the shriek of a pavement cutter, and with this a ripple of madness went through the park, the fountain coughed & sputtered, and *The Planet Saturn* increased in size.

TOWARDS THE SOUTH

During the Hot Season, in a section of the park saturated with *Magical Thought*, I abandoned my vows, and, heading south, set out to erase the line between man and beast.

EDGE OF THE PARK

All along the edge of a tin-pan park, my words rang hollow, and as annoyance turned to anger, and the first formations of a general uprising took shape, I thought it high time to quit the environs of Washington Square!

PELL STREET

In an apothecary window, nestled among antlers, hooves, and Ibex horns, was a manual of Taoist instruction: *The Seven Miracles of the Jade Stalk*. However, as a modest man of little ambition, I thought to myself that a single miracle ought to be more than sufficient!

ARTIFICIAL PARADISE

In order to amplify the natural *Blessings of the Fountain* in Washington Square Park, I consulted a magical plant: the strengthener of body & mind, as necessary as meat & drink!—I refer, of course, to the flowering tops of Cannabis Spontanea!

SPIRITED MOMENT

At the edge of a surging fountain in Washington Square Park, I expelled the entirety of my knowledge in a single burst of words, and thus depleted, felt bound to remove myself from *The Conversation of Man*.

THE CONVERSATION OF MAN

In the aftermath of *An Unconditional Surrender*, I headed south and retired to a bench of profound obscurity, where I felt confident that no information could reach me.

GOSPEL OF PHILLIP

Following in the footsteps of a certain Galilean Magician, I walked into the south west quadrant of Washington Square, where I obtained the ingredients for an unguent of remarkable curative properties.

HYPOTHETICAL AFTERNOON

On a hypothetical afternoon in August, as I passed through the vapors of the south west quadrant of Washington Square, I was given good reason to believe that the men of this region understood the use of drugs.

A REGION IN THE ATLANTIC

In an Aqueous Park, the rain drops hit the page of *Notebook No. 5,* and blurred my thoughts, which now seemed to emanate from some region in the Atlantic, a world submerged under its sorrows and vices.

THE PATRON GOD OF THE CITY

Irked, aggravated, and un-smiled upon by *The Patron God of the City*, I headed south, in search of a corresponding tier in the scaffolding of society.

DUST

Amid the horrors of The Renovation, in a roped-off section of Washington Square, I brooded upon things dusty, I brooded upon things past ...

UNACCEPTABLE EVENING

On an unacceptable evening, as tourists streamed through Washington Square, it seemed to me as though the whole of the park was raised to an intolerable pitch!

THE DESTRUCTION OF WSQ

As a pavement cutter tore open the crust of Washington Square, the jugglers scattered like ten-pins, the tourists fell back, and all manner of deceased and discarnate figures wandered about in great confusion.

UNMOVABLE BENCH

Somewhere south of the fountain, in a whirling, frantic park,
I sat alone, and bristled, and cursed the blustering crowd.

NEPTUNE

Under the faint light of Neptune, in a posthumous section of Washington Square Park, I came upon the skeletal remains of The Old Fountain, laid out across the brittle pages of *Notebook No. 37.*

MEDITATION

Somewhere in the deep recesses of spiritual fraud, I stilled my mind, and watched, with some irritation, as one moment succeeded upon the next.

ORNAMENTAL EVENING

On an evening of uncommon electrical activity, when respectable matrons darted about wild-eyed and lascivious, when mild-mannered fellows engaged each other like gladiators, and the likelihood of carnal activity became a near certainty, with electric steps I stole about the *Electric City*, and entering Washington Square, I strung the park with strands of colored lights!

ALL-PURPOSE PLANT

In a ritual already ancient in the time of the *Rig Veda*, seeking direct access to God, I made a pact with a plant of both fibrous and medicinal properties.

FRESH NOTEBOOK

From somewhere in the deep recesses of philosophy, with comments, observations, and rhetorical flourishes, I defiled the once-pristine pages of *Notebook No. 55*.

WELSHMAN

In an effort to broaden my knowledge of *Inner Alchemy*, and advance my spiritual standing, I switched from an Indian system to a Chinese one.

AMBIVALENT MAN

On the last day of The Mooncake Festival, in a remote area of Chinatown, I tarried on the doorstep of a restaurant for such an inordinate length of time, that they refused me entry, and wouldn't allow me to leave either!

INCREMENTAL IMPROVEMENT

In an effort to cleanse my spirit body, I shout silently every time an evil thought arises: Shut up! Shut up! Shut up!

THE RENOVATION

No, I don't see any of my *Old Classmates* along Washington Square West—I lost them all, a good half-century ago, though their shades remain. Alas! The past swirls around me like the dust storms that plague the park...

CLEANSING BREATH

As I inhaled deeply, I seemed to draw air from every obscure corner in Washington Square, and upon exhalation, rid myself of every obnoxious character in the park!

SPIRIT BODY

In the interests of alchemical research, I set about creating an etheric double of myself, but it began to develop ideas of its own, and soon became my mortal enemy!

FALSE HEARTH

All along the cold streets of a *Silent Night* city, every lighted alcove, doorway, shop, and store promised, for a moment, the warmth of hearth and home.

DISHONEST BENCH

Aggravated, and at odds with myself, I retired to a dishonest bench in Washington Square Park, where I frowned my approval, and applauded my displeasure.

SCAFFOLDING OF SOCIETY

During the whole of a scabrous night, driven like a dog through plywood pass-ways, I resigned myself to a city composed entirely of scaffolding!

BORDERLINE

In a borderline restaurant on the edge of Chinatown, at a table in the back, I scrutinized a greasy menu, and arriving at a decision, conveyed it to the waiter, who seemed to go along with it without too much fuss.

IN THE ELEVENTH MONTH

In the eleventh month of a lull in my employment, I remained steadfast in my belief that it is a man's misfortune that drives him to servitude, and not his faults.

IT DOESN'T SEEM FAIR SOMEHOW

In the wake of an overdue rent and unpaid electric bill, I concluded that real events of an appalling nature were being imposed upon a largely imaginary man.

THE TOWER

Upon a Purple Evening, underneath the Arch, I watched a sky-aspiring tower rise up south of Washington Square Park.

THE GRINDING DAYS OF DESPOND

That's how it goes these days: I'm scattered all through-out the park!—Yes, that's how it goes in the grinding days of despond !

THE FOUNTAINEERS

When *The Season of Fatigue* comes upon Washington Square, the Fountaineers—perhaps on a whim—often pump in waters from the Congo River, bringing with them all the characteristics of that terrifying body of water.

ELEVATED STATE

In a swollen Summer Park, my head grew large, and believing myself several spheres above the multitude, I spent the remainder of the evening on a bench built upon a raised platform, where I could be seen from any point in the city.

NECROMANTIC PARK

As disaster fell upon us, at last the Old Park was gone, and only the most obscure incantations and exotic drugs can bring it back again.

NIGHT TENT

In a ragged circus tent, in a corner of the night, unconvinced by dancing ponies, and acrobatic clowns, I bristled in my seat, and cursed the lusty, cheering crowd.

REMOTE RESTAURANT

In a remote Chinese restaurant, over Chow Mei Fun, I found myself assigning various qualities to the waiter: a grand benevolence, an overarching empathy, and a warm patriarchal concern, even though he appeared to be my junior by several decades!

ARTIFICIAL SPEECH

In a cordial section of Washington Square, as I wooed the crowd in pleasing tones, they at length became indignant, rose up and chased me round the fountain, and out of the park!

INNER RING

In the inner ring of the fountain, I told a woman everything I knew, then stood there depleted, while she gathered her things and withdrew.

A CONSIDERABLE MAN

Across the arid wasteland of my journals, among worries and weather reports, lie scattered fragments of myself—indeed, if we were to assemble them all, we might have the makings of a considerable man!

RUN-ON SENTENCE

All along the length of a run-on sentence in Washington Square, in the face of a strong head-wind, I laid out the whole of my philosophy, and upon completion, fell back into torpor and despond.

TRASH FIRE

During the dry season in Washington Square, as I wandered through a smoky section of the park, the truth was born upon me that all things of the world are consumed in the sacrificial fire of time.

AROMATIC SMOKE

In the aftermath of a rainstorm in Washington Square, from points around the park, there appeared certain half-familiar phantoms, and clouds of aromatic smoke.

POINTED INSULT

Yes, I am delicately and precariously put together, liable to be smashed into a thousand pieces by a casual remark—not to mention a pointed insult!

MULBERRY STREET

Over a span of several years, whenever I patronized the Pho Bang Restaurant, I invariably ordered the same dish: No. 39: Chicken w/Ginger & Scallions on Rice, until one day—before I could speak—the waiter asked: "No. 39?" I nodded my consent, enjoyed the meal, and didn't return for two and a half years!

ENGAGEMENT

Under an airy constellation, and a secret, potent drug, I threw off all restraint, arose, and exchanged pleasantries with a few people in Washington Square Park.

DISTURBANCE

When I enter certain restaurants, a tremor ripples through the room, and the waiters look askance as they wave me to the back, where I sit alone, insulted, intent on Beef Chow Fun.

ASYMMETRICAL AFTERNOON

On an asymmetrical afternoon in Washington Square, confounded with melancholy, and threatened by *The Ordinary Circumstances of Living*, I opened *Journal No. 37*, and inscribed the following entry:

> "All public parks are uninhabitable, unreachable, unthinkable!"

THE MACEDONIAN

In the Chess Plaza in Washington Square, on a High Summer afternoon of great anticipation, The Macedonian was preceded by rumors of his immanent arrival. As afternoon rolled away, still, the players held out hope, but when, at last, the shades of evening stole the light, and the royal game was done, no one would quite admit that The Macedonian would not arrive that day.

SKELETAL MOON

As a *Skeleton Moon* rose over the Chess Circle in Washington Square, my sense of self began to weaken, I grew afraid, and every table in the circle became a court of law where I was sure to be arraigned.

UNDERGROUND

As the city became more urbanized, I became an inconvenience to The City Planners, and in 1998, I was moved underground. The effort was successful, as all visible evidence of me seems to be gone, but if you know where to look, there are still traces of me in the city today.

ALL THE CLOCKS

In Washington Square, on an afternoon when all the clocks in the city had stopped, I climbed the three steps to the Raised Plaza, turned to the crowd, and told them I'd had enough!

HYPOTHETICAL ENCOUNTER

On an inconclusive day, on the far end of a ragged calendar, I found myself embroiled in the give & take of a hypothetical encounter, where I once again failed to hold my own—Yes!—I lose even when I am in control of the narrative...

AFTER TWILIGHT

In Washington Square, soon after twilight, having got together what was requisite for such a journey, I left The Holley Circle with the intention of reaching the Chess Plaza by nightfall. Arriving—much older now, of course—I stepped into that caustic crater with five dollars in my pocket, where I was welcomed like a dear and long-lost friend.

INCANDESCENT MOMENT

Upon exposure to sunlight, the disagreeable *Journal No.7* seemed to throw off its troubles for one brief moment before sinking back resigned, into the cold shades of uncertainty.

LOST AFTERNOON WASTED

Up from the moldering pages of *Notebook No.7*, through strife and cornball cracks, there arose the sick-room smell of a lost afternoon wasted.

BY NIGHT, ALONE

Fuelled by the potent oil of Hellebore, Cannabis, and Lupine, by night, alone, I stole along *The Achaemenid Royal Road*, on an errand of the utmost obscurity.

QUARTAN FEVER

I am King Xerophytus, the draught-resistant king, who rules over the land of the two rivers, who made the four corners of the earth obedient, and whose kingdom encompasses the entire zodiac!!!

AMMONIACAL CLOUD

In the famous outdoor lavatory of the Raised Plaza in Washington Square, I was overcome by a chemical cloud of such malignancy, that the tourists fell back, the rats gave notice, and the drunkards groaned in an uneasy sleep.

SUBTLE RESTAURANT

Today I dined in a restaurant that had gone out of business some time ago, and while I wouldn't necessarily recommend it, I will say that it possessed a certain elusive quality that I couldn't quite put my finger on.

UNHOLY PLACE

Staggering through the ruins of my childhood, I came upon the shell of the old RKO Keith's, and was sickened when a worker crawled out a second-story window, as if a worm emerging from a rotten fruit—I turned and fled from that unholy place!

EXTRA APARTMENT

In the third year of an *Inner Alchemy* experiment, I succeeded in creating an etheric double of my tenement apartment, but I soon lost control over it, and now all manner of unsavory characters live there!

LANTERN FESTIVAL

In a far corner of Chinatown, during the Lantern Festival, I found myself in front of one of those enigmatic restaurants that are neither open nor closed, as if they didn't want to tip their hand either way, perhaps fulfilling the terms of some strange and nebulous lease...

UPDATED EDITION

The Great Ledger of Unredressed Insults is a massive, weighty, ponderous, and terrible tome—updated editions appear daily upon my shelf: a publishing phenomenon!

DOWNTOWN

Aware that skin color becomes darker as one proceeds from north to south, I looked forward to reaching The Battery, where I would reunite with my people: the dark & gold-colored *Children of the Sun.*

OFF-REGISTER AFTERNOON

On an off-register afternoon in Washington Square, aggravated, and displaying a wide range of symptoms, I sank back into a bench in an uncharted warren of the park, and exhaling, resigned myself to the cold shades of obscurity.

MARGINALIA

On a lost evening in March, as I scanned the unpleasant pages of *Journal No. 5,* I found myself possessed by the fantastical jottings of a *Marginal Man,* and proclaimed them as my own!

RESTORATION

Somewhere along the far side of a disaffected dream,
I traced a circle in chalk where the Old Fountain
had been.

SCHEMATIC OF THE SELF

All along a bookshelf, I pursued an age-old forlorn hope: if only there existed somewhere, a *Schematic of the Self*.

THE LODESTONE

In search of an explanation, in a forlorn corner of the night, I stole into the Circle, and underneath the sand, I found a pulsing lodestone: the guiding lantern of the park!

MESOPOTAMIAN NOTEBOOK

On an agitated afternoon in Washington Square, well-vexed, and badgered by jazz-bands, jugglers, and acrobats, I opened *Mesopotamian Notebook No. 1* to an arbitrary page, and came across the following entry:

> "They did not hesitate to tear down the pious and loving work of previous kings."

Believing this to be relevant to our present dilemma, I book-marked the passage, and copied it into *Journal No. 37.*

SMOKE! SMOKE?

In a section of the park saturated with magical thought, I purchased two poems, a painting, and several sacred songs!

DIABOLICAL MARVELS

Among the diabolical marvels of the Chess Circle, is the hustler's habit of conferring an identity upon the passing tourists in the park: Chess playah! Chess playah!

HIGH PRIEST

On behalf of the community in Washington Square, I drank a sacred cup, and now all concerned pursue me, and seek out my advice.

THE BELLS

I thought I heard an insult, I thought I heard a jape—but no!—'twas just the baleful tones of *Journal No. 7*, tolling in my head.

IDEALIST

Somewhere in the deep recesses of disquiet, I stole from bench to bench, searching for an ideal place from which to vent my spleen.

INSOMNIA

In search of that deep, refreshing sleep that *The Ancients* spoke of, equipped only with an unguent box, and a pouch full of medicine, away from the prying eyes of The Inquisition, I wandered alone, through *The Ruins of Glaphyrae.*

DEPT OF COMPLAINTS

All about the building, there rose complaints about a stench, but no one guessed the source: the dead-rot at the core of *Journal No. 7!*

MOTT AND BAYARD

As I entered Mr. Tang's, a tremor travelled through the room, the cashier blinked, the waiter frowned, and waved me towards the back!

REPRIEVE

Across the long-haul of a dreadful sleepless night, as I weighed my every sin and indiscretion, and given up all hope of rest, at length there appeared a loathsome, mutant horse-head on a rotting merry-go-round: At last! The healing balm of sleep!

LATELY

Lately, the past has become inaccessible, untrustworthy, as perilous as the present, it won't behave like it used to, and can't be counted upon as a sanctuary—who knew the past would end up like this?

WHAT ABOUT A CITY?

What about a city whose IQ is fifteen points below the norm?—I might be able to flourish in such a city, and rise to a position of power...

DEEP BREATHING

In the after-tow of a tidal-wash, on a rotting bench
I sat, breathing complaints and imprecations into
Notebook No. 6.

END OF THE FESTIVAL

And then the wind turned blue, and whipped around the paths, and blew the people away like litter: the detritus of the park.

A PASTEL-HUED ALHAMBRA

All through the vagaries of a troublous, toxic sleep, laboring under the chronic state of mental dread in which *The Mesopotamians* spent their days, I searched for the luminous and long-missing Pastel-Hued Alhambra.

A SMALL CITY

I made a small city in my own image, and it's something I regret, and now I have to see myself in every doorway, store, and street.

DISCONTENTED EVENING

On an evening of discontent, after wandering through a warren of misbegotten streets, muttering incoherent prayers and casual complaints, I delivered myself to the cryptobiotic confines of Apartment No. 1—Yes, this is my home, gentlemen—Make sport of it, as you will!

CANNIBAL MOON

In Washington Square, during the dog days, a Cannibal Moon, milky, swollen, and intent on mischief, rose slowly over the old Chess Circle, and reaching its apogee, caught me in its sick and spidery light!

CHANCE ENCOUNTER

Pursued by all & sundry, I darted down the block, when a sullen fragment of my face accused me from a passing window pane—I turned away, I looked ahead, and hurried down the street.

192

END OF THE SEASON

In the dying *Days of Summer*, as I languished on a bench, a rude and rancid moon arose, and mocked me where I sat.

EXTRA EVENING

On an extra evening, I sank deep into a bench in Washington Square, and surrounded by suffumigations, reflected upon *The Golden Age of the City*, when learning, wisdom, and politeness flourished in Washington Square Park.

NOTHING TO BE DONE

When I see myself in a photo, mirror, or passing window pane, I say, well, alright then—this explains it: there's nothing to be done!

PSEUDONYM

In the purgatory of my private journals, I place people's names in quotes: "Bob", "Bill", "Jerry", and "Joan"—because I suspect that their identities are as false and flickering as my own.

JUST BEFORE THE FLOOD

On a night spent under Saturn, there crept into my mind, the troublous passing fancy that we presently reside upon *The Continent of Atlantis*—just before the flood!

WHAT ABOUT A MAN?

What about a man of indecision, who sat upon a bench? That's it? That's all? That doesn't tell us much!

IN THE CHALK CIRCLE

In a suburb of disquiet, around myself and the seasoned crew, I traced a magic circle in chalk, and bought myself a little more time ...

Made in the USA
Middletown, DE
18 November 2022

15399623R00125